DATE DUE

Cookie Crazy!

Adapted by Gail Herman from the television script
"Clifford's Cookie Craving" by Baz Hawkins
Illustrated by Steve Haefele

**Based on the Scholastic book series
"Clifford The Big Red Dog"
by Norman Bridwell**

SCHOLASTIC INC.

New York   Toronto   London   Auckland   Sydney
Mexico City   New Delhi   Hong Kong   Buenos Aires

JPICEZ

Copyright © 2003 Scholastic Entertainment Inc.
All rights reserved. Based on the CLIFFORD THE BIG RED DOG book series
published by Scholastic Inc. ™ and © Norman Bridwell.
SCHOLASTIC and associated logos are trademarks
and/or registered trademarks of Scholastic Inc.
CLIFFORD, CLIFFORD THE BIG RED DOG, and associated logos are trademarks
and/or registered trademarks of Norman Bridwell.

ISBN 0-439-47316-0

10 9 8 7 6 5 4 3 2   03 04 05 06 07

Printed in the U.S.A.
First printing, April 2003

Contents

🦴 Big and Red

Clifford The Big Red Dog loved being red. He loved being big. He stood way above everyone on Birdwell Island.

Each day he took his owner, Emily Elizabeth, for a ride all around the island. She sat on his back, and they went to the beach or the park or to visit friends.

They never worried about the weather. When it rained, Clifford

raised his paw and Emily Elizabeth
ducked under to stay dry.

If it got too hot, Clifford wagged
his tail. His tail was like a giant
fan. It cooled Emily Elizabeth off
right away.

One morning, Clifford set off by himself. "I wonder what T-Bone and Cleo are doing," he said.

T-Bone and Cleo were Clifford's best dog friends. "I'll go to T-Bone's house first."

"Surprise!" said Cleo when Clifford peeked into a second-floor window. "We're both here!" The purple poodle grinned.

"Hi, Clifford." T-Bone came to the window, too. "Guess what Sheriff Lewis brought me!"

Sheriff Lewis was T-Bone's

owner. And he was always bringing home surprises.

Clifford peered at T-Bone. The bulldog was jumping up and down, wagging his tail. He was very excited.

"A new bag of Tummy Yummies?" asked Clifford.

"Nope," said T-Bone.

"Doggy Doughnuts?"

T-Bone shook his head.

"Puppy Pancakes?"

"Enough already!" Cleo laughed. "It's not food. T-Bone has a new toy."

A New Toy

T-Bone held up a red ball for Clifford to see. "It's a big red ball," he said. "It reminds me of you, Clifford."

Clifford looked at the ball. It didn't seem very big to him. Still, his friends thought it was special.

"Wow!" he said. "Let's go play with it."

Cleo and T-Bone carefully climbed out the window. They stepped onto Clifford's head.

"Wheeeee!" They slid from his head to his tail — all the way to the ground!

T-Bone dropped the ball in front of Cleo. She pushed it with her nose. Then T-Bone rolled around on top of it. Faster and faster. He giggled as the ball spun and spun.

That looks like fun, Clifford thought.

T-Bone swatted the ball to him.

Clifford curled himself around the ball and tried to roll. Just like T-Bone.

Pffffft! The ball lost its air. It collapsed, flat as a pancake.

"I'm sorry, guys." Clifford hung his head. "I squashed it."

"That's okay, Clifford," Cleo said quickly.

"Don't worry," said T-Bone. "We can always get another toy."

But Clifford could tell they were disappointed.

"Maybe one day we'll get a giant ball," he said. "Then I can really play!"

🦴 Doggy Ride

Just then, loud music filled the air. *Ta-ra! Ta-ra! Boom! Boom!*

T-Bone clapped his paws. "Where is it coming from?"

Clifford gazed over the houses. "There's a marching band around the block. It's coming our way."

Minutes later, the musicians marched past. A group of children trailed behind.

"It's a parade!" said Cleo. "Is there a holiday today?"

"I know what's going on!"
Clifford said. "Today is the
Birdwell Island Fair. Emily

Elizabeth will be there. And Mr. Howard is going to take pictures."

Cleo nodded. "The band must be heading to the fairgrounds."

"The fair sounds like fun!" said T-Bone. "Let's go!"

Beep! Beep! Sheriff Lewis parked next to the dogs. He was driving a shiny patrol car. T-Bone leaped up to the open window. He licked his owner's face.

"I'm going to the fair," said Sheriff Lewis. "Do you want to come? I'll even sound the siren."

"Yip! Woof! Arf!" the dogs barked happily. In a flash, T-Bone and Cleo hopped in through the back window.

Clifford tried to follow. He stuck his nose inside. But the rest of him wouldn't fit.

"Oh, Clifford," Sheriff Lewis said. "You can run next to us."

"Woof!" Clifford barked yes. He took off next to the sheriff's car. *RRRRRRrrrrr!* went the siren.

In the backseat, Cleo and T-Bone barked. The wind blew their fur. It was so much fun!

Clifford was having fun, too. But
it would have been nice to be
inside the car, closer to his friends.

If only the car were as big as a truck. Then he could fit, too!

Soon Sheriff Lewis stopped by the fairgrounds. "Everyone out!" he said.

Cleo and T-Bone jumped out and landed next to Clifford. *Ta-ra-ra! Boom! Boom!* The parade marched past.

"Come on!" said Clifford.

The dogs followed the musicians through giant open gates and into the fair.

They were ready for anything!

🦴 Food Rules!

Clifford gazed at all the people, rides, and booths.

"Wow!" he said. "This is fantastic!"

Cleo and T-Bone jumped on his paw for a better look.

Flags blew in the breeze. In one corner, a big Ferris wheel turned and turned.

People played games like ring toss and "guess the number of jelly beans." All around, delicious smells floated through the air. Food stands lined every aisle.

Cleo took a deep breath. "Ahhh! There's nothing like the smell of popcorn in the morning."

T-Bone sniffed. "There's so much food!"

Cotton candy. Hot dogs. Burgers. Ice cream. Clifford couldn't believe all the good things to eat. This was going to be great!

Cleo and T-Bone were thinking the same thing. They leaped from Clifford's paw, taking off.

"Just remember our people-food

rule," Clifford called to them.

Screech. The dogs stopped. They turned back to Clifford.

"If it drops on the ground, or it's headed that way . . ." Clifford began.

". . . it belongs to the dogs, and that's okay!" Cleo and T-Bone finished.

Clifford smiled. "What are we waiting for?"

Searching for Snacks

Cleo and T-Bone raced off in different directions.

Right away, T-Bone spotted something interesting. A man was eating a hot dog. The man took a bite from one end of the bun.

"Oops!" said the man. The hot dog slipped out the other side.

T-Bone watched it fall down, down, down. Then it bounced up, up, up. Right into T-Bone's mouth!

"Mmm-mmm."

Cleo was following a group of children. They were walking and talking —  and eating popcorn. When popcorn fell to the ground, Cleo ran to get it. She scooped up the popcorn like a vacuum cleaner.

"Great idea!" said T-Bone, falling in next to her.

Clifford joined them a few seconds later. Soon the popcorn buckets were empty.

"All done!" he said happily.

"Shh!" said Cleo. "Look!"

A little girl was sitting in a stroller. She held a triple-scoop ice-cream cone.

Yawn! The girl was falling asleep. The cone tipped over. One scoop rolled off — right into Cleo's mouth!

The cone dipped lower. The

second scoop dropped. "Got it!" whispered T-Bone.

Then the last scoop wobbled . . . and wobbled some more . . . then fell. Clifford bent low and caught it.

"This must be dog heaven!" said Clifford as they walked away.

Cleo wagged her tail. "Let's see what else we can find!"

🦴 The Giant Cookie

On the other side of the fair, workers were setting up an exhibit. Above their heads, a crane held a tent in the air.

"Okay." Sheriff Lewis directed the workers. "Over to the right. Over to the left."

The workers rolled a giant sugar cookie onto a stand.

Mr. and Mrs. Bleakman stood nearby, watching. "Good job!" Mrs. Bleakman clapped her hands.

Just then, Mr. Howard walked
by. He took one look at the giant
cookie and stopped. "Wow, Mrs.
Bleakman. You baked quite a
cookie!"

Mrs. Bleakman grinned. "Oh, I
didn't bake it. Mr. Bleakman baked
it. All by himself!"

Mr. Bleakman nodded. "It's a beauty, isn't it?"

"It's the biggest cookie I've ever seen at the fair," Sheriff Lewis said.

"It has to be a prizewinner," Mr. Howard agreed. He raised his camera. "How about a picture, Mr. Bleakman? Cook and cookie?"

"Why, sure," Mr. Bleakman said proudly. He stepped close to the cookie and beamed.

Snap!

"Thanks, Mr. Bleakman."

Sheriff Lewis waved to the crane driver. The driver nodded. Then he dropped the tent in place — right over the cookie.

"We'll raise the tent at the end of the day," Mr. Bleakman explained. "Then everyone will see the cookie."

"Boy, will people be amazed," said Mr. Howard. He and the sheriff started walking away. "See you then!"

Mr. Bleakman took Mrs. Bleakman's hand. "Now I'm going to win you a big, stuffed teddy bear."

Mrs. Bleakman smiled. "That would be wonderful. But we should stay here and watch your

cookie. It smells so
wonderful.
Somebody might
want to —"

   "Oh, I'm sure
no one will bother it," Mr.
Bleakman said. He led his wife
away from the tent. "It will be just
fine."

🦴 Follow That Smell!

Clifford, T-Bone, and Cleo were still nosing around the fair. They stopped in front of a big taffy machine.

T-Bone licked his lips. "Mmmm. Sticky, yummy taffy."

The dogs watched the machine pull the taffy. This way. That way. Clifford felt a little dizzy.

But then he smelled something else. Something even better.

Clifford sniffed. "Do you guys smell that?"

Cleo and T-Bone lifted their noses. "I sure do!" said T-Bone.

"Scrum-dum-delicious!" Cleo said.

Clifford had to follow that scent. "Let's go!" he said.

The smell led the dogs past the pizza booth . . . the doughnut table . . . the hamburgers cooking on a grill . . .

Right up to a tent on the other side of the fair.

"It's coming from in there," said T-Bone. They all stuck their heads under the tent.

A cookie! Clifford gasped. And what an amazing cookie!

He wagged his tail so hard, flags flapped in the wind. Hats flew off heads. Cotton candy blew off sticks. Pinwheels spun wildly.

"Wow!" said T-Bone.

"That's one big cookie!" said Cleo.

Clifford's eyes grew wide. It *was* big. Not like the toy ball he'd squashed. Or the police car he couldn't fit into.

"It's just my size!"

🦴 Cookie Crazy!

Minutes passed. The dogs couldn't stop looking at the cookie. It was the most amazing thing!

Finally, T-Bone and Cleo shook their heads. They turned away from the cookie.

T-Bone shrugged. "Well, it's not on the ground."

"And it's not headed that way," Cleo put in.

Then T-Bone and Cleo said

together, "So it's not for the dogs
and it's not okay."

But Clifford didn't say a word.
He just kept staring. It was like the
cookie had him under a spell.

"Uh-oh," said T-Bone. "Maybe
we should get out of here."

Cleo noticed Clifford, too. He
had a funny look on his face.
"Right," she said. "Let's go."

Cleo and T-Bone wiggled out of the tent. But Clifford was rooted to the spot. He didn't move.

Cleo tapped him. "Clifford? We need to go now."

Clifford still didn't move.

"Come on, big guy," Cleo said a little louder. She scooted back

inside the tent. She waved her paws in big motions.

Clifford didn't even look at her.

"Clifford has gone cookie crazy," said T-Bone. He crawled inside, next to Cleo.

Cleo nodded. "Well, it's the first time he's ever seen a cookie that big. It's his size."

"He's got to forget about it!" said T-Bone. "And we've got to help!"

Cookies Everywhere!

Cleo and T-Bone led Clifford to the other side of the fairgrounds. A flying disk lay on the ground. T-Bone picked it up.

"How about a game of catch, Clifford? That should take your mind off that cookie!"

T-Bone flung the disk. Cleo leaped into the air. She caught it in her mouth.

"Here it comes, big guy!" Cleo shouted to Clifford.

Clifford nodded. But he wasn't
really listening. *A big treat must be
for someone big*, he told himself.
And I'm the biggest someone I know.

"Clifford! Heads up!" yelled
Cleo.

"Huh?" Clifford looked up. The

disk was flying right at him. But he didn't see a disk. He saw a cookie.

Clifford bit the disk. *Snap!* It broke in half. "Mmmmmm."

"Clifford?" Cleo said. "You're eating our toy."

It was a toy? Not a cookie? Clifford spit out the disk. "Oops! Sorry, guys."

"You've got to get your mind off that cookie, Clifford," said Cleo.

"I'm trying, Cleo. . . ." Clifford trailed off. In the distance, a man was selling balloons. But Clifford didn't see balloons. He saw sugar cookies floating in the air. "But everywhere I look, all I see are big sweet cookies!"

Clifford spotted the Ferris wheel next. In a flash, he took off running.

Cleo and T-Bone raced after him. "Clifford, come back!" they shouted.

"I've just got to have it!"
Clifford said, still running.

"Stop!" T-Bone shouted.

Clifford stopped. "Huh?" He
looked at Cleo and T-Bone. Then

he looked back at the Ferris wheel. "Oh," he said. "It's only a Ferris wheel."

Cleo shook her head. "Poor guy. He has a bad case of cookie-itis."

All at once, a breeze blew. It carried the cookie smell right up to Clifford's nose. A silly grin spread over his face.

"Clifford?" said T-Bone.

"Clifford?" said Cleo.

Clifford didn't answer. In a daze, he sniffed and sniffed. And he ran — right to the cookie tent.

ᴥ Let's Eat!

There it was! The giant cookie! It looked just as yummy as it did before. So delicious . . . so chewy . . . Clifford couldn't see or think of anything else.

Clifford was half in the tent and half out of the tent. The tent was too small. But that cookie . . . that cookie . . . was just right.

"I know I shouldn't eat it," he said. "And I won't. I just want to look at it. And maybe take one little sniff. . . ."

He put his nose close to the cookie.

Just then his friends wiggled into the tent. "Clifford!" they shouted.

Surprised, Clifford jumped. His nose bumped the cookie. *SNAP!* Off came a big chunk. It fell to the ground with a thud.

The dogs edged closer.

"Wow!" T-Bone said. "A piece of cookie is on the ground."

"It was an accident!" Clifford said.

Cleo eyed the giant cookie crumb. "You know the people-food rule. If it drops on the ground . . ."

"Or it's headed that way," T-Bone put in.

"It belongs to the dogs," said Clifford, "and that's okay!"

Clifford's eyes grew bright. "That's the rule. So let's eat!"

🦴 How to Fix a Cookie

T-Bone and Cleo looked at each other. They nodded. "You can have it, Clifford," said T-Bone.

"It's all yours," Cleo added. They knew how important it was to Clifford.

"Really?" Clifford picked up the cookie chunk. "Thanks!"

He chewed a few times, then gulped. "Mmmm!" He smiled. "That was so good!"

Then T-Bone glanced at the

cookie. "Gee, it looks kind of funny now. It's missing a big piece."

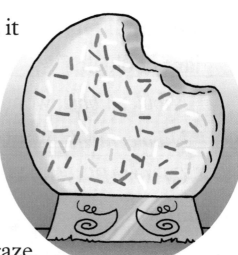

Clifford followed his gaze. It was true. The giant cookie was uneven.

"I know!" said Clifford. "We can eat all around the cookie. We'll even it out. That way, nobody will notice a piece is missing!"

It seemed like a good idea to Cleo and T-Bone, too. The dogs stood in different spots around the giant cookie.

Nibble, nibble, went T-Bone.

Nibble, nibble, went Cleo.

CHOMP! CHOMP! went Clifford.

Finally, they stopped. Cleo and T-Bone were so full their bellies sagged to the ground.

"That was a tough job," said Cleo. "But it had to be done. And we were just the dogs to do it!"

"I can't eat another bite!" T-Bone said. He yawned.

"Me, neither," Cleo said in a sleepy voice.

"Uh, guys?" Clifford gazed at the cookie. "Doesn't it still look funny? A little lopsided?"

T-Bone and Cleo slumped to the

ground. "Maybe a little," Cleo said. She closed her eyes.

"We'll have to eat some more," said T-Bone. He tried to stand.

"That's okay," Clifford told them. "You've helped enough. I'll fix it myself!" he said bravely.

🦴 The Tent Goes Up

A crowd stood by the cookie tent. Emily Elizabeth, Mr. Howard, and almost everyone from Birdwell Island were there.

Mr. Bleakman faced them. Sheriff Lewis sat in the crane. He was ready to raise the tent.

"Ladies and gentlemen," Mr. Bleakman said. "Get ready to see the biggest sugar cookie ever! A real Clifford-sized treat."

Emily Elizabeth laughed. "He's

right," Mr. Howard told her. "Just wait until Clifford sees it."

Sheriff Lewis pulled a lever. The tent lifted up a bit. Everyone leaned forward to see.

There were Cleo and T-Bone, fast asleep.

The crane lifted the tent higher.

And there was the cookie stand . . . but no cookie! Just a big red dog.

Everyone gasped. "Clifford!" Mr. Bleakman said, shocked.

Clifford jumped to his feet. He

saw the empty cookie stand. He didn't mean to eat the whole thing!

Emily Elizabeth ran to him. "What happened, Clifford?" she asked.

Clifford whined. He was so sorry!

Mr. Bleakman's face turned bright red. "That big red rascal ate my cookie!"

Everyone Makes Mistakes

Mrs. Bleakman rushed over to her husband. She patted his arm. "Now, now, Horace. You can't really blame Clifford, can you?"

"What?" Mr. Bleakman asked.

"Well, you made a delicious-smelling . . ."

Mr. Bleakman nodded.

". . . yummy-looking . . ."

"True, true," Mr. Bleakman said.

". . . crunchy-sounding . . . scrum-dum-delicious cookie!"

Mr. Bleakman smiled.

"How could the poor dog help himself?" Mrs. Bleakman finished.

Mr. Bleakman closed his eyes. He pictured his giant cookie. "It was beautiful, wasn't it?"

Emily Elizabeth stepped closer. "Oh, Mr. Bleakman!" Her voice trembled. She felt so bad. "I'm so sorry Clifford ate your cookie. And I know Clifford is very sorry, too."

Clifford dropped his

head close to Mr. Bleakman. He put his paw over his eyes. Then he peeked out.

"Well," Mr. Bleakman said slowly. "It *was* a pretty great cookie. I can't blame Clifford. He saw something that was just his size, and he couldn't help himself. Everyone makes mistakes sometimes."

Mrs. Bleakman reached for his hand. "Even you make mistakes. Right, Horace?"

"Yes, Violet," said Mr. Bleakman with a smile. "Even I make

mistakes. Like leaving that big cookie near a very big dog."

Clifford licked Mr. Bleakman's cheek.

"Okay, okay. I forgive you." Mr. Bleakman sighed. "I just wish there was some way everyone could have seen my cookie."

Mr. Howard stepped forward. "I think I know a way."

The next day, an even bigger crowd stood by the cookie tent. A big photograph of Mr. Bleakman and his cookie rested on the stand.

"It's a real winner," said Mrs. Bleakman.

Clifford leaned closer. He sniffed the picture.

"And do you know the best part?" said Mr. Bleakman. "I can leave *this* cookie alone. Even with Clifford around."

"Woof!" Clifford leaned closer to the picture. It looked so yummy. So big. So Clifford-sized.

Clifford wanted to nibble it. But he wouldn't make that mistake ...ce!